For Bella Jean, Laurel and Carla –
inspirational big sisters! AMQ
For Christine and Charlie, RB

First published in paperback in the UK in 2013 by
Alanna Books
46 Chalvey Road East,
Slough, Berkshire, SL1 2LR

www.alannabooks.com

ISBN: 978-1-907825-05-7
Printed and bound in China   PB1

Lulu reads to Zeki

Anna McQuinn
Illustrated by Rosalind Beardshaw

ALANNA BOOKS

Lulu's day always ends with a story.

Tonight, her mummy reads one about a little girl and her new baby brother.

Lulu's mummy is having a new baby, too.
Lulu is going to be a big sister.

Mummy's tummy gets bigger and bigger.

But she still has time to read with Lulu.
Lulu chooses stories the baby will like.

Daddy makes new shelves for the baby's things and Lulu sorts her books.
Some are for keeping...

...and some are for the new baby. She puts them on the new shelf with her duck and her old teddy.

Then one day, the new baby arrives.
His name is Zeki.

Lulu brings him a soft book for his cot.
It's a perfect present for a new brother!

Lulu's new baby brother cries a lot!

Lulu wants to cheer him up
so she tells him a story.

But it turns out he is
just hungry.

So, while Mummy feeds Zeki, Lulu holds
her best bear story.
She and Mummy read it together.

Sometimes Zeki cries when
he needs a new nappy.

Lulu reads him her best potty book.

Sometimes he cries in the bath.

Lulu reads him her best duck story.

Sometimes Zeki cries when he's tired.
Lulu reads him her best sleepy story.

She sings a song for Zeki and then he goes to sleep.

Lulu's new baby brother sleeps a lot!

While he is sleeping Lulu plays
with her teddies.

Being a big sister is a big job.
Sometimes Lulu helps her mummy.

Sometimes she helps her daddy.
The new baby keeps everyone very busy.

But they are not too busy to end the
day with a story...

...for the best big sister of all.

alanna books
because everyone loves a good story...

Little Frog learns that his family love him eventhough he is very naughty.

Paperback: 978-0-9551998-68

Boys do not play with dollies! Girls do not play with aeroplanes!

Hardcover: 978-1-907825-026

A tender, funny story about an unlikely friendship.

Paperback: 978-0-9551998-99

Can the friendship survive a new addition?

Hardcover: 978-1-907825-088

Lulu loves going to the library – she chooses new books, enjoys story time and joins in with singing. And every night her mummy reads her a story. Look out for the new hardback edition with free CD. The paperback edition also comes with a free multi-language CD. Listen to the story told in over 20 languages - perfect for inclusive story times. The board book edition is shorter with simpler text, making it perfect for younger children.

Hardcover & CD: 978-1-907825-071

Paperback & CD: 978-0-9551998-20

Board book: 978-0-9551998-75

Irish language Edition
Paperback & CD: 978-0-9551998-82

Lulu and her daddy read a different story every night and next day, Lulu acts out the characters and storylines. The paperback edition comes with a free multi-language CD. Listen to the story told in over 20 languages - perfect for inclusive story times. The board book edition is shorter with simpler text, making it perfect for younger children.

Lulu has a new baby brother. Whenever he's upset, Lulu reads him one of her favourite stories.

Hardcover: 978-1-907825-051

Paperback & CD: 978-1-907825-019

Board book: 978-1-907825-022

Hardcover: 978-1-907825-040

Paperback: 978-1-907825-057

www.alannabooks.com